FROM SHEEP TO SHORE

FROM SHEEP TO SHORE

WRITTEN BY PHILIPPA ROBINSON-GILL
ILLUSTRATIONS BY ADAM GILL

Matador
Unit E2 Airfield Business Park,
Harrison Road, Market Harborough,
Leicestershire. LE16 7UL
Tel: 0116 2792299
Email: books@troubador.co.uk
Web: www.troubador.co.uk/matador
Twitter: @matadorbooks

ISBN 978 1803132 914

British Library Cataloguing in Publication Data.
A catalogue record for this book is available from the British Library.

Typeset in 20pt Latin Modern Roman by Troubador Publishing Ltd, Leicester, UK

Matador is an imprint of Troubador Publishing Ltd

This book is dedicated to my four-legged friends, Brock, Bramble, Floss, Meg and Jack, who have given me so much love, affection, amusement and exercise, and without whom, I would be twice the size I am and half as happy.

On a green field high up on the hills above their farmyard home, two Border collies are working hard running left and right, moving sheep down through the fields towards the barn at Brock Farm.

Meg, with her sleek, smooth coat and large, pointy ears, is small but fast, dazzling the sheep with her rapid turns, making sure none of them take off in the wrong direction.

Jack, her brother, is much bigger, with a thick, wavy coat, big squishy paws and a long, bushy tail. What a wonderful team they make: Meg, using her speed and quick thinking, Jack with his great size and enthusiasm.

The sheep on the farm have dense, grey wool fleeces to keep them warm in the cold, snowy weather that arrives each winter on the hills.

Now summer is here, their coats are too warm and heavy, making them uncomfortable.

The farmer has decided today is the day the sheep need to come into the barn to have those woolly fleeces shorn off.

The flock have had their wool clipped and are looking much cooler.

All except one...

Fraser the ram!

He is by far the biggest and most stubborn sheep on the farm.

If they want him to go left, he goes right; if they want him to come out of the barn, he goes in.

Both dogs creep slowly behind him, heads down, bottoms up, barking encouragement.

As Fraser runs through the large, heavy barn door, he gives it one enormous, bad-tempered kick with his strong back legs.

The door shudders and crashes shut; Meg cannot jump out of the way fast enough, and it hits one of her legs.

Limping badly, Meg lies down on the straw, whimpering...

Weeks later and Meg is still holding her paw a little off the ground as she runs.

She isn't as quick as she was, struggling to do her fast turns.

It's difficult for Jack to move the sheep on his own, particularly the awkward Fraser.

The farmer decides he'll need to get another dog to help with the flock and find Meg a new home where she doesn't have to work anymore.

The farmer has an idea and rings his sister Claire.

Claire and her husband Jim live in Seaglass Cottage, a cosy little house which, most importantly, has a long, sandy beach and the sea at the bottom of the garden.

Claire is delighted to take Meg in and immediately says, "Yes! It's different from the farm and the sheep, but I think Meg will love it here."

Living by the sea is magical, with so many new things for Meg to see and sniff; even the air smells somehow different; when the wind blows, it makes Meg's nose twitch and wrinkle but all in a good way.

Gazing out at the clear, blue sea that never stops moving and the long, golden, sandy beach, Meg feels exceedingly small, and even though she has started to make friends with some of the dogs she has met on the beach, sometimes, like now, she feels something is missing.

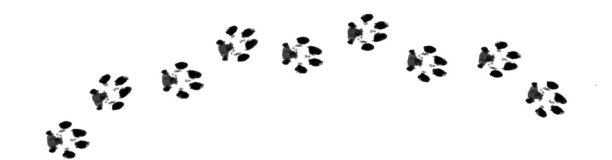

A few weeks later, Meg is asleep in her soft, warm basket, legs twitching rapidly as she dreams of gathering sheep in the fields with Jack.

In her dream, Fraser the ram refuses to go into the pen with the others, and Meg barks at him to move along, waking herself up with a start.

The sheep had always been hard work, nothing like her life now by the sea, where every day brings something new and exciting.

If only her brother Jack could be here. There's plenty of space for another basket in the house and masses of room on the beach.

As Meg lies there, she suddenly thinks she can hear Jack's deep bark, but surely, she must still be dreaming...

Just then, Jack rushes into the room, his big, bushy tail tickling her ears as he brushes past, bouncing with nervous excitement and running in circles round the room.

"Someone said beach – what's a beach?"

"Jack! What are you doing here, and who's looking after the flock?" Meg exclaims, laughing.

Jack says, "Oh, they've gone; the farmer has cows now which are much bigger, even bigger than Fraser, and they've long, curved, sharp horns...

"I do not like cows; they don't listen to me. I'm a sheepdog not a cattle dog, so the farmer said I could come live with you by the beach."

Both dogs stand up to look out of the large front window.

Meg's very excited and can't wait to get out there and show Jack the beach with the enormous castle hidden in the dunes and the sea that has a bright lighthouse rising out of the waves.

Jack, however, cannot help feeling a little nervous inside as he looks out.

Being a big dog, he doesn't want to show Meg how nervous he is, but it looks so different to the hills and fields he's used to.

Meg runs to the door barking, but Jack lies down in the hallway looking on, undecided as to what to do.

It doesn't take long for his curiosity to get the better of him, and when Claire opens the door, the two dogs sprint down the garden towards the soft, sandy beach.

Everything feels new and a bit scary to Jack: the sand beneath his paws which shifts a little as he runs, the people carrying brightly coloured deckchairs, babies wriggling in their pushchairs eager to get out and the many big, white birds in the sky with their strange, laughing voices.

Children are busy on the beach making sandcastles of all sizes; using their brightly coloured buckets and spades, they scoop, pack, tap and jiggle the moist mix out of the upturned buckets and cheer as each new castle appears.

Jack can see a small group of children standing around a particularly elaborate sandcastle, decorated in seashells and pebbles with brightly coloured flags fluttering on top.

Some of the children carry buckets filled with seawater, ready to fill the deep moat they have dug all around their sandcastle.

Jack stops and stares, wondering which way to go; he does not want to get too close to the children or their sandcastle.

Meg isn't looking at the children or their sandcastles; so overjoyed to be with Jack again, she is turning circles on the sand and running backwards, keeping her eyes on Jack as much as she can.

Walking backwards is something Meg is normally really good at; she often does it when she is watching Jim to see where he will throw her ball.

People point at her and comment on how clever she is, but today, in her excitement, she is running not walking and definitely not concentrating!

The children move away to admire their wonderful sandcastle, now complete with a water-filled moat. Just then... *Kersploosh!*

Meg tumbles backwards straight into the water. Scrambling as quickly as she can to get out, she steadies herself before giving a big shake and running on, hoping Jack hasn't seen her embarrassing fall.

Stealing a glance behind her, she sees the children are gathered around, staring at a pile of sand with a flag sticking out of it where the castle used to be...

Now running side by side towards the shore, Jack sees more water than he's ever seen before.

He steals a look at Meg, who is holding a blue squeaky ball in her mouth which he didn't notice before.

Meg isn't scared, and Jack is so pleased to be back with Meg and chasing after the ball, trying to get to it before she does, he forgets all about being nervous.

After playing in the waves for an awfully long time, Jack is hot and thirsty, and he needs a drink. Surrounded by all this water, he thinks being thirsty isn't a problem and takes a big gulp out of the sea.

Meg has seen him and tries to bark a warning but isn't quick enough... Jack coughs and splutters, trying to spit out the water as fast as he can.

He doesn't understand – this isn't like the water on the farm! This is salty, very salty... yuk. Meg can't help laughing. "Perhaps now is a good time to go home," she says.

Walking up the front garden path, Meg spots Belle and Bert, the little tan terriers that live next door.

As usual, they are sitting in their upstairs window.

They are wearing colourful bandanas around their necks; Belle's has purple and yellow spots, while Bert's is blue and green checked.

Meg nudges Jack. "Look up there – that's Belle and Bert, but I call them 'The Watchers'."

"They sit in that window all day watching what is going on.

"They'll have spotted you, Jack, the new dog on the beach."

Jack looks up and gives them what he thinks is his most appealing smile, hoping 'The Watchers' will be his friends.

He has never had friends who wear bandanas before, particularly not as colourful as those.

Seeing Jim at the open front door, Jack dashes past, giving a vigorous shake of his long, wavy coat as he goes by, showering both the floor and Jim in sand.

"Oh, Jack, you're bringing the beach into the house," says Jim, laughing.

Waiting for them in the kitchen is a really big bowl of their favourite biscuits and refreshing clean, clear water that definitely doesn't taste salty!

In the front room there is now not one cosy-looking basket but two.

Looks like Jack, like Meg, has gone from sheep to shore, and Meg could not be happier.

Soon asleep in their baskets, both Meg and Jack dream – I think you can guess what they dream about...

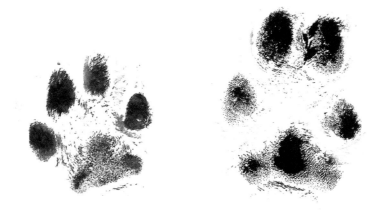

ACKNOWLEDGEMENTS

My greatest thanks and admiration go to my very talented brother, Adam Gill – without his wonderful, inspirational illustrations and design, this book would never have come to life. Thanks too, to my extended family who supported me with their endless patience, advice and encouragement, for which I am very grateful. Thanks also to Tony (alias Jim) for his unwavering support and belief in me, which enabled me to make a dream come true. Lastly, special thanks, pats and hugs to our much-loved Meg and Jack and all their four-legged friends who entertain me each and every day.

MEG AND JACK'S BIOGRAPHY

Border collies, or sheepdogs as they are more commonly known, are extremely intelligent, very energetic and enthusiastic dogs that love to herd sheep, cattle or occasionally even ducks. Both Meg and Jack's working life on the farm was quite short but for different reasons.

Meg was four when she came to live with my husband and I by the sea in Northumberland. Already a mum, she had lost some of her interest in looking after the sheep and was happy instead to watch her daughter Nell and son Patch working with the farmer as they skilfully moved the sheep around the fields. One day, I happened to call on the farm where she lived and met this extremely sweet, big-eared girl and suggested she might like a home by the sea with no work to do but lots of space to run and play, and home she came.

Jack was one of three brothers born on a hill farm like the one in the story; even as puppies, they were big and very boisterous. Now one year old, the farmer was struggling to train them all at the same time and was looking for someone who could give one of them a lovely home away from the farm. Meg came with us in the car when we went to see the brothers, and on opening the door, Jack jumped straight in and sat beside her in the basket – I think he chose us.